Long Long Time Ago

Korean Folk Tales

Illustrated by Dong-sung Kim

Elizabeth, NJ·Seoul

Long Long Time Ago

First published in 1997
Revised edition, 2008
Second printing, 2010
by Hollym International Corp.
18 Donald Place, Elizabeth, New Jersey, 07208, USA
Phone 908 353 1655 **Fax** 908 353 0255
http://www.hollym.com

Hollym

Published simultaneously in Korea
by Hollym Corp., Publishers
13-13 Gwancheol-dong, Jongno-gu, Seoul 110-111, Korea
Phone +82 2 734 5087 **Fax** +82 2 730 8192
http://www.hollym.co.kr **e-Mail** info@hollym.co.kr

ISBN: 978-1-56591-254-0
Library of Congress Catalog Card Number: 97-74945

Printed in Korea

Long Long Time Ago

From the times immemorial, folk tales and stories have delighted children everywhere. Children are most happy when they are listening to stories into sleep, and living the stories in their dreams. Sometimes the stories make them feel happy, sometimes sad, weak or strong, scared of brave, but mostly the stories make them grow. Children who read lots of stories can learn how to behave, what is more important, how to dream, how to make their dreams come true, and how to sympathize with others.

Here in these 20 most wonderful stories, you will meet the long-time friends of Korean children. A rabbit who outwits a tiger, a brother and a sister who became the Moon and the Sun, ogres and their magic clubs, a tortoise and a hare who are totally different from the ones in Aesop's fable, rats who want the sun to become their son-in-law, and many many more beloved characters.

Such stories as these, while appealing to children everywhere, are true reflections of Korean customs and tradition at the same time. So they sure will serve as a fantastic way to understand the culture and customs of Korea.

KOREAN FOLK TALES IN THIS BOOK

Mr. Moon and Miss Sun

A long time ago, there lived a little brother and sister with their mother in a small cottage deep in a valley far, far away.

One day, their mother went to another village to help prepare for a great feast. The children had to stay home alone and watch over the house. Their mother finished her work as soon as she could and started out for home, but the sky had already become dark.

As she went over the first hill, the children's mother was suddenly startled by a big tiger. The tiger roared, then walked up and sniffed her. She was very frightened indeed.

"If you give me a rice cake," said the tiger, "I won't eat you."

She quickly threw the tiger a piece of rice cake and started to run. The tiger ate the rice cake in one swallow and dashed to the next hill. When she reached the other side of the next hill, the tiger was already waiting along the path in front of her.

"If you give me a rice cake, I won't eat you," said the tiger in a deep voice.

The poor woman threw the tiger another piece of rice cake and started to run again.

The tiger swallowed the rice cake at once and raced ahead of her.

At each hill he waited for her, growling, "If you give me a rice cake, I won't eat you."

Before long, she had given the tiger the last of her rice cakes. So the next time the tiger said, "If you give me a rice cake, I won't eat you," she had no more to give, then the tiger ate her all up.

It became darker and darker, and finally it was night. The children were very worried, but still their mother didn't come home.

The girl said to her older brother, “I’m scared. Where is Mother?”

As the boy was older, he thought he should try to smile, then said, “Don’t worry. She’ll be home soon. Let’s wait a little longer.”

Just at that moment, they heard a loud noise. Someone was trying to open the door latch. Then they heard a voice saying, “Children, open the door. It’s your Mother.”

“Oh! It’s Mother!” said the little girl. She jumped up to open the door. The boy grabbed her. “Wait!” he said, “That does not sound like Mother’s voice.”

Then, “I caught a cold and my throat is sore,” said the voice from outside. “Stop playing around and open the door.”

The boy held his younger sister tight. He was not sure what to do.

“Show me your hand,” he shouted.

A big, shaggy, yellow paw pushed through the paper window.

“That’s not Mother’s hand!” cried the girl.

Hearing this, the voice outside said, “I worked very hard today. My hands are all rough now. Stop playing games and open the door right away.”

The children still hesitated to open the door.

“You must be very hungry. I’ll make you something to eat,” said the tiger as it hurried into the kitchen wearing Mother’s clothes.

The boy felt bad. “Poor Mother,” he thought, “I’ll help with supper.”

But when he walked into the kitchen, he saw a tiger’s tail coming from under his mother’s dress.

"It's a tiger!" he told himself.

Quickly and calmly he led his little sister outside.

"That's not Mother in the kitchen," he told her. "It's a tiger! We have to hide."

Together they climbed up an old tree by the well. Back inside the house, the tiger was warming himself by the fire of the kitchen oven.

After resting there for a while, he licked his lips and said to himself, "It's time for supper. I'm going to make a nice little meal out of those two kids."

Then he flung the kitchen doors open. But the house was completely empty.

"Where did my supper run off to?" the tiger wondered.

He ran through the house, turning over the furniture and breaking the dishes as he looked for the two children.

Then he happened to see the girl's shadow move.

"Ah-ha! They climbed up the tree. How silly they are!" the tiger muttered to himself.

"Children!" he called up at them. "What are you doing climbing trees at night? You could fall and hurt yourselves! Get down here this instant!"

The little girl began to tremble with fear, but together the children stayed up in the tree.

The tiger then set about climbing the tree to catch them. Every time he got halfway up the tree trunk, he slipped back down to the ground.

"How did you two climb up there?" the tiger shouted from below. "The tree is so slippery that your poor old Mother can't climb it. Come down this moment!"

The boy decided to play a trick on the tiger. "It was easy, Mother. Get some sesame oil from the kitchen and rub it all over the trunk."

The tiger believed what the boy said, so did exactly as he was told. He brought a big jar of sesame oil from the kitchen and spread it all over the trunk of the tree. Then he tried to climb the tree again, but of course the sesame oil made the trunk even more slippery than before. The tiger slid down to the ground hard and fast, landing right on his tail. "Ow!" he cried.

The girl could not help laughing. "Silly old fool!" she laughed. "If you used an ax, climbing the tree would be easy," she then added. Just as soon as she said this, the girl realized she shouldn't have spoken and stopped laughing.

But it was too late, for the tiger already heard what she had said. He found an ax and struck at the tree. Then he pulled the ax out and struck the tree agin, higher up this time. Using the cuts in the trunk as steps, the tiger was able to climb higher and higher up the tree.

The girl looked down at the tiger coming slowly up the tree and then looked up at the sky.

"Oh, Heaven, please save us," she prayed. "Please send us a rope."

Just as the girl had asked, a rope dropped gently down from the sky above. The girl and the boy quickly grabbed the rope and were pulled up away into the sky.

At exactly that moment, the tiger reached the highest branch of the tree. Watching the children disappear into the clouds, he became very angry. Repeating what he had heard the little girl say, he prayed, "Oh, Heaven, send me a rope, too."

A second rope dropped gently down to the tree. "Follow that rope!" the tiger roared as he grabbed on. The Heavenly rope carried the tiger high above the ground.

But the rope was rotten and snapped, sending the tiger falling to the earth below. Every bone in his body was broken.

The two children kept going higher and higher.

The boy became the Sun, shining brightly all day long. The girl became the Moon, lighting dark roads at night.

But the girl was very frightened and didn't want to be all alone at night. So her brother changed places with her and became the Moon.

Ever since that day, the girl was called Miss Sun and the boy was called Mr. Moon, and no one could look at the face of the once shy Miss Sun, because now she is brighter than anything.

The Son of the Cinnamon Tree

Once upon a time, there stood a very big cinnamon tree. Every time sweet smelling flowers bloomed on its sturdy branches, a fairy maiden would fly down from heaven to visit it.

The fairy would lean against the tree and sing in a lovely voice. The wind would scatter the tree's flowers and send the young maiden's song far, far away. The cinnamon tree loved to listen to the beautiful voice of the fairy. And the fairy loved to smell the fragrant flowers of the tree.

Soon the cinnamon tree and the fairy maiden got married and gave birth to a charming little boy.

The baby gradually grew into a strong young boy listening to his fairy mother's music and enjoying his father's fragrance. As soon as the boy grew old enough, the fairy left him with the cinnamon tree to go back to her home in the sky above.

In summer of the year she left, there was a great rainstorm. First the fields became covered with water. Soon even the mountains were buried in water. The tall cinnamon tree stood bravely on a steep hill, but it too was covered in water before long. Finally, it could no longer withstand the strong waves. It fell down with a loud crash into the rising water.

The tree shouted to the boy, "Quick, my son! Hop onto my back." So the boy jumped onto his father's bark-covered back.

The cinnamon tree and his son floated all around the world, which was by now completely covered by turbulent water.

As they floated about the world on the flood waters, they happened to see some ants floating in the water. "Save us. Please save us!" shouted the ants when they saw the tree passing by.

The boy felt sorry for the tiny ants. He asked the cinnamon tree, "Father, is it okay if the ants also ride on your back?" "Of course," answered the tree. "Help them get on."

So the boy picked all of the ants up out of the water and put them on his father's back. The ants bowed their heads in gratitude and said to the cinnamon tree, "Thank you, great tree. Someday we will repay you for your kindness."

After a short time, a swarm of mosquitoes came buzzing by. They pleaded with the tree, "May we mosquitoes also ride on your back?" "Of course," said the tree.

So the mosquitoes landed on the cinnamon tree and rested their tired wings.

A few days later, the boy saw another boy of his own age splashing about in the water, screaming for help. The boy asked the cinnamon tree, "Father, may that boy ride on your back?"

But, much to the boy's surprise, the cinnamon tree said, "No, he cannot." The boy begged his father, "Please let him come with us. If we don't help him, he will drown!" But the cinnamon tree said, "No! He cannot come with us."

Still, the boy kept pleading with his father.

Finally, the cinnamon tree gave in to him, "Okay. Do as you wish."

So the boy pulled the drowning boy from the water and helped him ride on the back of the tree.

For many days they floated all over the world. One day, they found an island at long last. The boys, the ants and the mosquitoes got off the tree's back to walk around the island, and the tree floated away to look for more land. The two boys found an old woman and her two little granddaughters living on the island.

The five were the only people left in the world at last, after many days of rain and clouds, the sky cleared and the water slowly began to dry up.

The two boys lived in the old woman's house and farmed the land.

The old woman liked the son of the cinnamon tree. He was very polite, kind and also hard working.

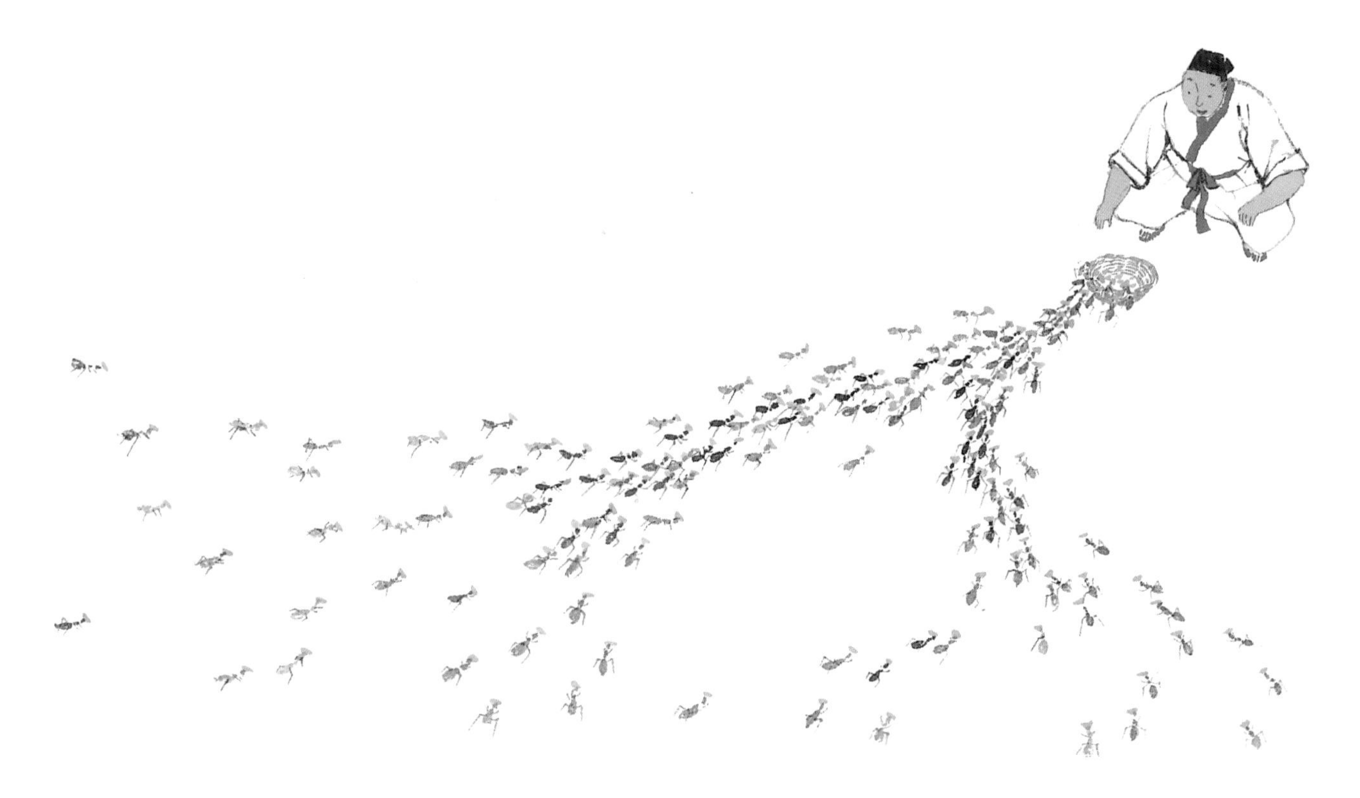

The other boy, who was none of those things, became very jealous of the cinnamon tree's son. He decided to make the son of the cinnamon tree look bad in the eyes of the old woman by telling her a lie.

"My friend is very clever," he said to her, "and he's so skillful that if you dump a basket of rice in a sand, he can pick out every grain of rice and put each one back in the basket."

The old woman was amazed. "Is that so? That's really amazing. Let's give him a try."

So she spilled a basket of rice in a pile of sand. Then she called the cinnamon tree's son to her and told him to go pick out the rice and put it back in the basket.

The boy went over to the sand and began picking up the white grains of rice. He worked very hard, but he couldn't even gather a single handful of rice.

Suddenly there appeared a group of ants. They began to pick up the grains of rice. In no time at all, they picked up every grain of rice and put it back into the basket.

Seeing the results, the old woman liked the cinnamon tree's son even more.

Before long it was time for the boys to get married. The old woman called the two boys and said, "The flood has made sure that there are no people left on this earth. You must marry and have many children. The house up on the hill has two rooms. One of my granddaughters is in the room on the east side of the house, and the other is waiting in the room on the west side. Choose one room and marry the girl inside."

The son of the cinnamon tree wanted to marry the girl who was smart and kindhearted. Just in time the mosquitoes he had saved during the flood came buzzing towards him. They whispered in his ear, "Go onto the room on the east side of the house. East, east, east ..."

The boy did as the mosquitoes told him. Inside, the smart, good-hearted young lady sat waiting with her head bowed. The boy married the girl and they lived very happily together.

The bad boy who had been saved from the sea went into the room on the west side of the house and married the girl who was waiting there. They lived many unhappy years with each other until they learned to treat each other with kindness and respect. Both couples had many sons and daughters.

This is how the world was once more filled with people.

The Herdsman and the Weaver

Once upon a time there lived a king who reigned over the Heavens. He had a lovely daughter that knew how to weave the most beautiful cloth in the world. The king would jokingly call the princess "My Weaver."

The princess's loom would rattle and knock all day long as the shuttle danced in and out among the threads. Seated there she would make them into cloth that would be the envy of any young woman. She spent her childhood there in front of that loom until it came time for her to get married.

The king searched his kingdom far and wide to find a suitor for his daughter.

One day he met a young man whom he liked very much. "This young man will make a fine husband for my daughter," the king told himself. The young man was a herdsman. He had loved cattle ever since he was a little child, so he was very happy with his work.

One beautiful spring day when all of the flowers were in bloom and the birds were singing, the weaver married the herdsman. All the king's subjects were overjoyed at the news.

After the wedding, the young couple spent all their time frolicking about the fields together.

The herdsman deserted his cows. Eventually the cows wandered into the royal garden, trampled all over the royal flowerbed, and ruined it. The weaver no longer wove any beautiful cloth. A thick layer of gray dust gathered on her loom.

When the king knew what was happening, he became very worried. He called the two lovers to him and said, "Son, you are still a herdsman. You must take good care of your cows!" Then he looked at his daughter and said, "You must not abandon your loom."

But the herdsman and the weaver had been married at a very young age and were still really just children. They didn't realize the importance of what the king was saying to them.

They kept roaming the fields and merrily playing games with each other.

The king became very angry this time. He scolded them at the top of his lungs, saying,

"How can you feed yourselves if you don't do any work? You have not obeyed me. I have no choice but to punish you."

Pointing at his son-in-law, he said, "From now on, the herdsman must live in the Eastern sky," then he turned to his daughter, "and the weaver must live in the Western sky."

When the herdsman and the weaver heard this, they both cried, "Oh, Father, please forgive us. We know we were wrong to play in the fields all day. We promise to do our share of work. Please let us stay together. We love each other more than anything!"

But the king was not moved by their tears. The herdsman and the weaver were forced to part. The herdsman went East and the weaver went West.

They were so sad that eventually the king began to feel sorry for them. Finally he decided to let them meet once a year on the banks of the Milky Way River.

All year long, the two lovers counted the days and nights thinking of meeting each other again. Both now realized that they had been disobedient to the king.

The day finally came when they were allowed to have their yearly meeting. With high hopes, each headed for their meeting place by the Milky Way River. But when they reached it, the river had become so wide and the night so dark that they could not see each other.

The herdsman and the weaver stood on the banks of the Milky Way River and cried. Tears rolled down their cheeks and into the river. The water from their tears flowed down into the river and became rain. The rain then fell to the earth until the ground was wet and soggy. The seas rose higher and higher.

The fields and gardens of the kingdom were flooded. Not only that, the homes of the king's subjects were swept away in the waves.

The animals of the kingdom became very alarmed indeed. They all met to decide what to do. Each animal took turns telling everyone at the meeting what they thought would be a good way to stop the flood of tears. Some made low grunts and some made high squeaks. Some of them whistled when they talked.

Finally one animal came up with a suggestion. "We must help the herdsman and the weaver get together again. Otherwise this rain will never stop."

"Yes," said another, "let's build a bridge for them!"

"That's it!" exclaimed another animal. "We must build a great bridge!"

All of the animals agreed. But none of them knew how to go about building a bridge, as animals don't usually know how to build bridges. They all lay around looking at one another, twisting their tails in silence.

Finally some crows and magpies chirped up. "Let us birds do it," said one. "We can fly to the Milky Way River," said another, "and make ourselves into a bridge."

So all of the crows in the world got together and made a big flock with their cousins, the magpies, and flew up to the Milky Way River. They flew tightly together, holding on to each other with their talons. Soon they stretched from one bank of the river to the other.

The herdsman and the weaver were very surprised to see a bridge of birds.

"What is this?" they exclaimed. "Now we can cross the Milky Way River and be together again!"

The herdsman and the weaver ran across the backs of the birds. In the middle of the bridge of birds they met and held each other in tight.

Right around this time the heavy rains slowed to a drizzle. But then the two lovers had to return to their homes in the East and the West for yet another lonely year.

After that, on the seventh day of the seventh moon of every year, all the crows and magpies would fly to the Milky Way River to form a bridge. The herdsman and the weaver would meet on that special day every year by crossing the river on the backs of the kind flock of birds.

Crows and magpies did not always loose their feathers once a year. Ever since they started forming flocks to fly to the Milky Way River, and ever since they started helping the herdsman and the princess see each other, they have lost their feathers after the seventh day of the seventh moon.

Now you know why everyone in the kingdom treats them kindly.

The Donkey's Egg

A long, long time ago, there was a farmer who lived deep in the countryside. He was a very kind man, but not very smart. The people in his village teased him because he was always doing foolish things.

One summer day, the farmer's wife gave him a bolt of cloth that she had weaved.

"Go to the market and look around real good," she said, "then sell this cloth and use the money to buy something we need."

Being a good husband, the farmer immediately headed for the market carrying the cloth on his back.

The market was full of people. There were many different kinds of goods in the market. The farmer went from one stall to another, looking for something that his wife would like. He sometimes would pick up something and look at it in his hands, even if it was something he knew he could not afford. Some merchants got angry. They told him to buy something or go away. But the farmer could not find anything that seemed very useful.

It was almost sunset before the farmer managed to sell the cloth his wife had weaved. Now that he had the money in his hands, he thought to himself, “It is getting late. I must make up my mind and buy something very quickly.”

He started wandering around the market again and searching for something useful to bring home.

He passed by a fruit stand. A huge basket of ripe watermelons sat in front of the stand.

“I wonder what these are,” he said to himself, as he had never seen a watermelon before. He called to the owner of the fruit stand. “Excuse me, sir. What are those big green round things out here?”

The owner of the fruit stand tried hard to keep from laughing out loud. He thought to himself, “What kind of fool doesn’t know a watermelon? I think I’ll play a little joke on this foolish stranger.” With a very serious expression on his face, the fruit stand owner looked at the farmer and said, “They are donkey eggs.”

The farmer reached down and touched one of the watermelons. He had a look of amazement on his face.

He opened his eyes wide and asked, "How does a donkey come out of the egg?"

The man selling the watermelons said, "If you put it on the floor near the kitchen stove and cover it with a blanket for one month, it cracks open and a baby donkey will come out."

So the farmer spent all his money on a watermelon.

He skipped all the way home as he thought, "A donkey for a bolt of cloth ... today's my lucky day!"

The farmer's wife greeted him warmly as he entered the house. "What did you buy?" she asked. "What do you have there?"

The farmer said proudly, "It's a donkey egg. If we put it by the stove and cover it with a blanket and leave it there for one month, a baby donkey will come out!"

"Wonderful!" the farmer's wife exclaimed, overjoyed at what her husband was saying.

"We'll have to cover it right away."

So she quickly went into the kitchen and made a fire in the stove.

The farmer and his wife counted the days until it was time for the donkey egg to hatch.

Finally a month had passed and the day they had been waiting for was at hand. The farmer and his wife threw off the blanket. Their hearts were beating with excitement.

"Phew! What an awful smell!" they both exclaimed. They covered their noses and cringed. The farmer shouted in anger, "What has happened? We did exactly as the fruit stand owner told us. Why did the donkey egg rot?"

The farmer took the rotten watermelon and threw it into the garden.

Now, there happened to be a baby donkey grazing on some grass behind a bush near the garden. It was startled when the farmer threw the watermelon, and ran out from behind the bush, braying loudly.

When the farmer saw the baby donkey running from behind the bush, he naturally thought that it had been hatched from the "egg" that he had just thrown away. He ran after the baby donkey.

When it ran into a neighbor's barn, the farmer followed it. Then a villager came out and yelled at the farmer. "What are you doing in someone else's barn?" The farmer kept in pursuit of the donkey. "I'm trying to catch my baby donkey that just hatched from its egg," he shouted.

When the neighbor heard this, he fell to the ground roaring with laughter.

The farmer finally managed to put a rope around the donkey's neck and take him home.

The farmer's wife petted the baby donkey. "I am going to weave a lot of cloth. Then we can buy more donkey eggs," she said.

Just then the real owner of the donkey happened to see it on the farmer's property and he became very angry.

"Hey, you!" he shouted at the farmer. "What are you doing with my donkey?"

When the farmer heard this he became angry, too. He shouted back, “This is my donkey. It hatched in my garden today.”

The villagers who had come out to see what the fuss was about all roared with laughter.

“That foolish farmer is at it again.”

The donkey’s real owner marched into the farmer’s barn and led the donkey away. The foolish farmer just stood there and watched.

The Ogres' Magic Clubs

A long time ago, there was a kindhearted young man lived in a small village. As on many typical village days, the man went into the hills nearby to gather some wood. After gathering a big load, he sat in the shade and wiped the sweat from his face. He was still resting when something hit him on the head.

"Ouch! What is this?" he said, looking at what had just fallen from the sky. "Ah, it's a hazelnut! Father would like this," he thought, putting it in his pocket as another hazelnut fell on his head.

"I'll give this one to Mother," he thought as he put the second hazelnut in his pocket.

Then two hazelnuts fell together, and the young man was elated. "Wow!" he said to himself. "This is my lucky day! These two nuts are for my older brother and me."

Although he didn't notice that the sun had started to set behind the mountain and that it was already getting dark, he did notice when a heavy rain started to fall. Quickly he jumped up and put the load of wood on his shoulders.

“Where can I hide from this rain?” he thought as he wandered around the mountains, with his feet slipping and sliding on the wet leaves.

Sliding around in the weather like that, he barely noticed that he had come upon a small cottage.

“Whew! At last I’ve found a place to rest for a while,” he told himself and went inside right away. The cottage was run down and looked as if no one had lived in it for a long time.

Soon, however, he heard something outside. It was the thump-thump-thump of heavy footsteps. The young man shook with fear. “What kind of people would live here? They must be thieves!” he thought, and quickly climbed up onto a beam high up in the roof.

Some shadows burst into the dark house and laughed among themselves.

“A-ho-ho-ho, a-hee-hee-hee ...”

When he looked down and saw them, the young man was so surprised that he almost fell off the beam. They were not people at all! They were a bunch of ogres, each with horns on their head. The young man shook with more fright now than he had before.

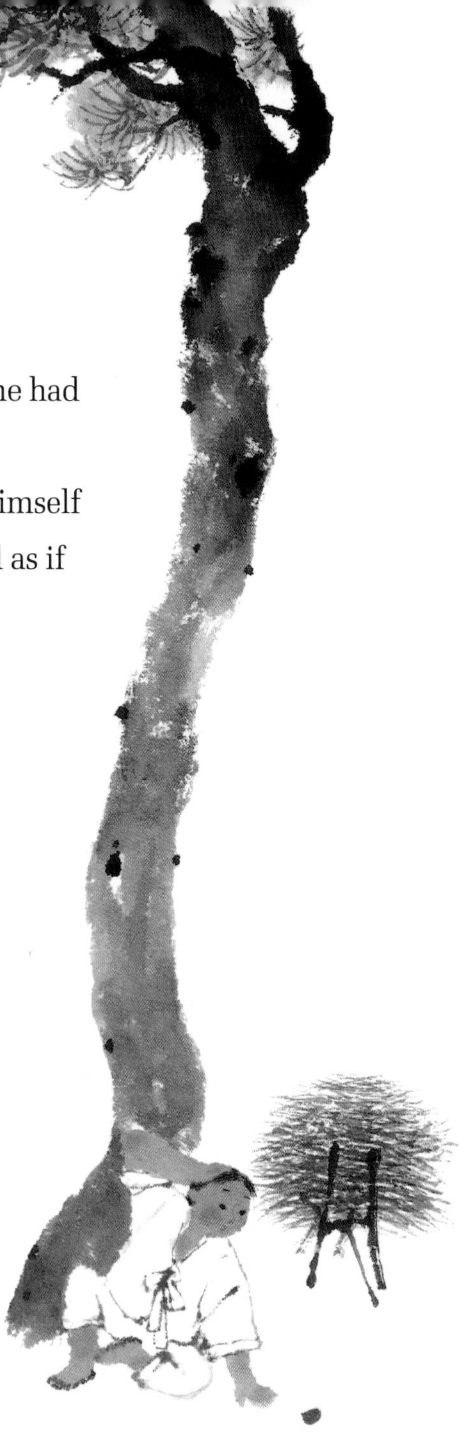

Then one of the ogres shouted, "Well, shall we begin our game?" Thump! Thwack! The ogres struck the floor with their clubs as they sang.

"Gold, gold, come ye forth!"

"Silver, silver, come ye out!"

Every time they hit their clubs on something, gold and silver coins shot out. The young man watched in fascination from just under the roof as they played their greedy game.

They were having so much fun that they started to skip about and dance, all the time singing their magic chant and striking things in the room with their clubs.

The young man had forgotten his fear, but this was mostly because he suddenly realized that he was quite hungry. Without thinking he took one of the hazelnuts out of his pocket and tried to break it open with his teeth. The hazelnut broke open. Crack!

The ogres stopped in their tracks. "What was that loud noise?" one of them exclaimed.

"Oh, we must have hit the floor too many times! The house must be falling down!" another cried.

"Hurry! Run! Get out of the house before it falls down on us!" yelled a third.

And the ogres all rushed out of the house as fast as they could.

The young man heard the ogres shout. And since he didn't know that it was his cracking the nut that had scared them, he was again frightened and confused. So, he stayed right where he was on top of the beam and slept there till morning.

He woke when the morning sun started to shine through the door, and it was only then that he finally decided to come down. The entire floor was covered with gold and silver coins.

"What foolish ogres!" he thought. They left without taking any of this with them. Just for fun, he picked up one of the clubs and hit it against the floor, repeating the song he had heard from up on the beam last night.

"Gold, gold, come ye forth!" he sang, and gold coins came pouring out. He laughed and decided to take the ogre's magic club home with him.

The young man became very rich. The wealthier he became, the more jealous his older brother became at the sight of all the gold and silver coins. His brother had always been both greedy and lazy, and was now raging with envy.

One day the older brother lazily wandered up the mountain to gather wood, just as his younger brother had done before.

When he got to the forest, he stretched out on the path and started to take a nap. He never tried to gather any wood for the family.

The sun descended in the sky. Suddenly a hazelnut from a tall tree fell with a thud right next to him and it made him awake.

"Hee, hee. This will taste good. I'll eat it later," said he as he put the nut in his pocket.

Another hazelnut fell to the ground. "Wow! Look at this!" he exclaimed. "Now I have another to snack on later!" he said as he put the second hazelnut in his pocket.

He kept sitting there, even though the sky was growing darker and he still had not gathered any wood.

When it got dark, the older brother got up and stumbled his way through the forest. He too happened upon the small, remote cottage in the woods.

Once he got there, he also climbed up on the beam and lay down to rest some more.

It wasn't long before a group of ogres rushed in from the dark. They all swung their clubs in the air and shouted, "Whoopee!" and "Hurrah!" as they sang and danced around the room.

"Gold, gold, come ye forth!"

"Silver, silver, come ye out!"

The ogres jumped about as they pounded their clubs.

The older brother watched the scene below with keen interest. Remembering the story his younger brother had told him, he suddenly had an idea. "If I crack open a hazelnut, it will scare away the ogres! Then I'll have all their clubs for myself!"

So he took a nut from his pocket and bit down on it with all his might. Just as he thought, it made a loud cracking noise as it spilt open above the heads of the ogres. When they heard the noise, they immediately stopped playing and stood still.

"I bet that is the man who tricked us last time," said one of them.

"Let's catch him!" shouted another, and they all started rummaging through the house.

The older brother tried to stay perfectly still on his beam. This wasn't easy because he was shaking with fear. Eventually one of the ogres saw him move.

"Ah-ha!" it shouted, "There he is!"

The older brother cried as he pleaded with them, "Please, please, let me go!"

"You foolish human," they shouted all together. "You stole one of our clubs, yet you still think we'll just let you go?" They looked at each other for a moment. "Let's give him a good beating."

After they beat the greedy older brother over and over, they finally decided to let him go alive.

That day the older brother went home sore in body but also much wiser. And he never went back to that shack in the woods again.

The Snail Lady

Once there was a young man who lived all alone in a small village. One day while he was hoeing his garden he muttered to himself, "Every day I hoe the fields and harvest crops. If only I had someone to share my meals with ..."

"Share your meals with me."

It was a woman's voice. The man was very surprised. He looked all around, but he could see no one. After a while he went back to hoeing his garden.

"Every day I hoe the fields. But who do I have to share my meals with? I'm tired of eating alone," the young man kept on talking to himself. Then he heard the woman's voice again.

"Share your meals with me," said the voice.

This time he noticed that the voice came from somewhere close by. The man looked at the hedge that separated the fields. All he saw was a small snail.

He couldn't find the source of the voice. Without thinking much about it, he picked up the snail and put it in a big clay jar.

When the man woke up the next morning, he found a delicious breakfast waiting for him. “Who could have made such a wonderful meal?” he exclaimed, with his eyes wide open with amazement.

That evening another meal lay on the table prepared for the young man.

“This tastes really good! Tomorrow I’ll have to hide and watch to see who is secretly making me these nice meals,” the young man thought to himself.

The next day he pretended that he was going out to work in the garden. Instead he noisily walked out of the yard, then quietly tiptoed back and hid near the kitchen.

Peeking into the kitchen, he saw something that at first he couldn’t believe.

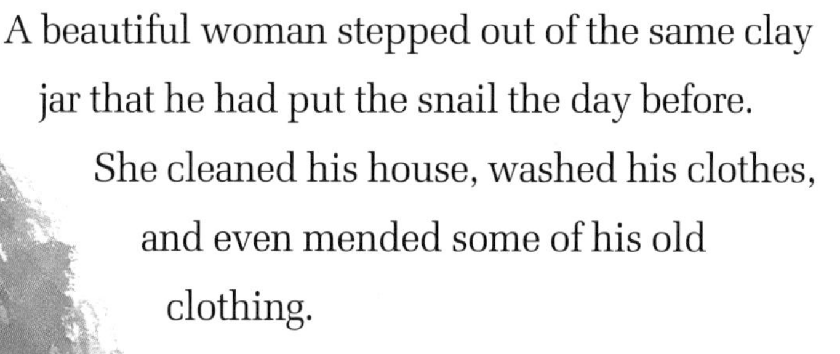

A beautiful woman stepped out of the same clay jar that he had put the snail the day before.

She cleaned his house, washed his clothes, and even mended some of his old clothing.

When evening came, the young woman prepared his dinner.

Then she turned into a snail and slowly crawled back into the jar. As the man stared in amazement, he thought to himself, “How I wish that beautiful lady were my wife!”

The next morning the man woke up early and sat by the jar. Before long, the snail lady crawled out. The man grabbed her hands tightly and said, “Would you please be my wife?” The lady blushed. Then she nodded, and the young man and the snail lady lived happily together as husband and wife for many years.

One day the king went hunting near the village where the happy couple lived. When the king rode his horse past their humble little house, he saw the beautiful snail lady standing outside.

“What a beauty!” he exclaimed. “How come she’s married to some farmer! I should make her my wife.”

The king was a very cruel and unjust king. He called to the young man, "I challenge you to a contest. Tomorrow we see who can cut down a tree faster. If you win, I'll give you half of my kingdom. But if you lose, you must give me your wife."

When the young man heard this, his face turned white.

The snail lady fastened a note to her wedding ring and gave it to her husband. The note said, "If you throw this ring into the ocean, my father, the Dragon King, will help you."

So the young man tossed the ring into the ocean. Amazingly, the sea spilt apart as the ring hit the water. Right at that spot a path appeared and it led down into the sea. At the end of the road stood the Dragon King's majestic castle. The young man went inside.

It was not long before the Dragon King appeared. Without saying a single word, the Dragon King, who was now his father-in-law, gave him a gourd. At first he didn't know exactly what the gourd was for, so he just took it home and waited.

When the day of the contest arrived, the king chose two trees for the contest. As he was a cruel and unjust king, he chose the smaller one for himself and the larger one for the young man. Then the king ordered two hundred of his finest soldiers to start cutting down the tree. He had an evil smirk on his face.

The dispirited young man did not know what to do. But holding his breath and praying hard, he cracked the gourd open. Out came countless little men, all with little axes in their little hands. Quickly they marched into action.

Together the little lumberjacks took their axes and started chopping away at the big tree with swift little chops. In hardly any time at all the little men had felled the young man's tree. The king's soldiers had gotten into each other's way so much that they didn't even get halfway through the little tree that the cruel king had chosen for himself.

But the king didn't keep his promise. Instead of giving the young man half of his kingdom, he thought up another way to try and win the snail lady.

"We must have another contest tomorrow. This time we'll race our horses, and the first one to cross the river wins."

Again the Dragon King said nothing when the young man came to the Dragon Palace in search of help. All he did was give his son-in-law a skinny, tired-looking colt.

The king mounted his tall, strong, regal-looking horse. Nearby the young man climbed the tired, weak-looking horse that his father-in-law had given him. Just before the young man was fully settled, the king started off across the river. Somehow the young man's horse

ran as fast as lightning and was on the other side before anyone realized it had won. The king got so angry trying to catch up that he fell into the water.

Of course the king did not keep his promise this time either.

"This time we'll race boats," said he, eager for another chance.

The young man got a small rowboat from the Dragon King and floated his way out into the ocean. The king sailed out in his shiny, sparkling new ship.

The young man's little boat shot ahead of the bulky royal ship so fast that even the king thought it was a dolphin. The king turned red and stamped his feet. He tried to think of another way to justify taking the beautiful snail lady away with him. He might have thought of something if a big wave didn't come up and swallow his ship.

Having beaten the king once and for all, the young man took the entire kingdom for himself. But he took the food and riches that the mean king had hoarded throughout his reign and gave them to the poor. All he wanted was live with his wife happily ever after.

The Lazy Man

Once there lived a young man who spent his whole day doing nothing. Even during the busiest time of the farming season, he just slept and snored while the rest of his small village went to work.

After years of waiting for the situation to improve, his wife could no longer keep her temper under control. In her loudest possible voice she yelled right at his ear, "Get out into the fields and do some work."

The man just rolled over on his side and frowned much like someone that had been suddenly awakened in the middle of the night.

"Don't bother me," he said. "Why do you keep bothering me when I'm so tired?"

His wife had heard him say this many times before, so became all the angrier.

"How can you spend a day sleeping? You're sleeping right through the peak of the farming season!" she complained. "Even our poor children go out to the fields to work. The whole family will starve to death if you keep on loafing around like this!"

The man held his hands over his ears and grumbled, "I'd be better off if I found somewhere else to sleep."

"Leave then! Now!" yelled his wife.

For once the man jumped out of bed and ran off. His wife was so surprised at the speed with which he moved that she just stood there with her mouth open.

The man was walking down the road when he saw an ox chewing its cud. It was half asleep, resting in the midday sun. He stood and looked at the ox with envy. He thought to himself, "If only I were an ox ..."

There was no shade along that part of the road, so he continued his stroll toward the ridge of a nearby mountain. When he reached the ridge, he saw a shanty with a straw roof. The hut was so old that it was barely standing.

Inside an old man was very busy making something. The lazy man stopped to look, not because he was envious, but he had never seen such an old man so busy working on something.

"Excuse me," he said to the old man, "what are you making?" The old man held up a mask and grunted, "I'm making an ox mask." The lazy man laughed at the old man. "A mask of an ox head? Why would anyone work so hard to make something so worthless? It would be far better to just sleep."

Now the old man laughed. He laughed a heartier laugh than the lazy man had. "There is no such thing as worthless work," he said. "Is that what you think?" asked the lazy man. "Well, in that case, good luck to you and your noble task."

As he turned to go, the old man grumbled softly, "This mask might come in handy for someone who doesn't want to work."

"Come in handy, you say? How?" the lazy man replied.

"If you really want to know, why don't you try it on?" said the old man as he quickly placed the mask on the lazy man's face. Then he tied a leather strap he had been hiding to the iron ring that went through the nose of the mask.

No matter how hard the lazy man pulled and pulled, the mask would not come off.

"Help me get this thing off!" he begged. "It's very hot." But his words sounded very strange. They were very low and gruff, not unlike the noise an ox makes. He made noises that sounded like "Moo! Moo!" The lazy man ran around in circles, bawling just like an ox. "Moo! Moo!" he cried.

The old man held the leather strap and led the lazy man away, ox mask and all.

Along the way, the lazy man heard the sounds of men laughing and arguing. From the smell he could tell that he was in the market where oxen were bought and sold, and that

he was fenced in a small area crowded with other oxen.

He could barely hear the old man talking to a local farmer. "Now remember," the old man said. "Make sure you keep him away from the radish fields. He'll die on the spot if he eats radish." Then he heard the farmer say "Some oxen sure are peculiar." Then the lazy man was led to a new home, just like an ox from the market.

It was the hottest part of an already very hot day. “Hurry up, you stupid ox! Why are you acting so lazy?” The farmer yelled as he hit the back of the lazy man with a big stick.

“I’m not an ox,” the lazy man complained. “I’m a man wearing a mask.”

But his words sounded just like the sounds an ox makes. So convinced was the farmer that he hit him even harder.

The man stopped mooing and thought to himself, “I guess this is my punishment for being so lazy.”

Once at the farmer’s house, he worked all day long. He even had to pull a heavy wagon!

When the sun had set at the farmer’s house, the lazy man was led to his new pen. He was very tired, but he couldn’t sleep. All he could do was cry and think about his family.

"I wonder how my wife and children are," he cried. "I'd rather be dead than be an ox," he said to himself.

Suddenly he remembered what he had heard the old man tell the farmer while he was being sold at the market. "That's it! I'll eat some radishes!" With what little strength he had left, the lazy man broke out of the pen.

He went over to where the farmer had left a basket of radishes and picked up a hoof-full. "So this is what it's like to die," he said. Then he closed his eyes and bit down hard on a radish.

Just as he did this the ox mask fell off his face. "What's happening?" he wondered out loud. He was so happy he didn't know what to do. Soon the ox hide fell off his back and he was a man again.

He was still there when the farmer came out to feed his animals.

"Hey! What's going on here?" the farmer shouted at the lazy man. The lazy man was so happy to be a human being again that he actually tried to explain the whole story to the farmer. Then he headed back to his family.

Once home, he set out to work in the fields and worked hard all day. His wife never discovered the reason for the change in her husband. But from that day on, he was known as the hardest-working man in the village.

The Fountain of Youth

Once upon a time in a high mountain village, there lived a good-hearted old man and his wife. Mostly they were very happy, but sometimes they were sad because they had no children. Even though they loved each other, they felt a little lonely and empty.

Every day the old man went into the woods to cut wood to sell as firewood when the market opened. Cutting wood was not easy for someone of his age.

One summer day, a day that seemed no different from any other, the old man went into the forest to cut wood, just as he always would on a normal day. On this day, however, the old man heard the beautiful sound of a bird singing.

"That must be the loveliest sound I have ever heard!" he exclaimed. So, just for a moment, he stopped chopping and wiped the sweat from his forehead.

Then the sweet song of the bird became even more impressive. "Tweet, tweet, tweet."

The song was so beautiful that the old man decided that he had to see the bird. He put down his ax and went over the hill, following the sound as he went.

Soon he came upon a strange white bird that was perched on the branch of an oak tree. The old man had never seen a bird quite like it. He was awfully tired, so sat down to relax to the song being sung by the strange bird. But it flew over to a tree a little ways off and started singing a different tune.

The old man still wanted to hear more, so he walked up to the tree the bird was singing from and sat down again.

But just as he sat down, the bird stopped singing and again flew to a tree just a little farther off and then started to sing once more. For the third time the old man wandered over to where the bird was singing.

The bird kept going deeper and deeper into the woods.

Before he realized it, morning had become afternoon. The old man suddenly looked all around him. "What have I done!" he cried. "Why have I wandered so far? Where am I?"

Almost as if it had heard what he had said, the bird flew over to where the old man stood scratching his head in wonder. It circled around the man's head a few times, then landed beside a nearby spring.

The old man was very thirsty from walking so deep into the forest. He bent down and drank some spring water by making a cup with his hands. "This is very refreshing!" he said to himself between swallows. "It's as sweet as honey!" But then suddenly he felt very lightheaded.

"Why do I feel so strange?" he wondered. "I feel like I've been drinking wine." The old man lay down on a smooth rock and fell fast asleep.

The day grew dark but the old man didn't return home so his wife became very worried. Surely he hasn't run into a wild animal, she tried to assure herself.

When it became too late to put off her fears any longer, the old woman went searching all around the neighborhood for her husband.

But he was sleeping soundly on a rock in the deep, deep forest. He didn't wake up until it was the middle of the night. "What am I doing sleeping here?" he said to himself. Quickly he hurried back out of the forest.

After looking here and there for her husband, the old woman finally went to the house next door. "My husband is lost in the mountains," she said, "I'm afraid something has happened to him. Can you help me find him?"

But the man next door was known throughout the village as a very selfish person. "Look here!" he said in an angry voice. "It's the middle of the night. It's no time to go looking for someone. I'm not going anywhere."

The old woman had no choice but to set out on the treacherous path alone.

She had not gone far when her husband came running toward her. They hugged each other until they cried. Then they walked back home, arm in arm.

Inside, the old woman lit a lamp. As soon as the room lit up, she almost fainted.

"Who are you?" she screamed.

"It's your husband, of course," the old man said. "Is something wrong?"

The old woman slowly backed away from her husband, "Are you some kind of ghost?" she asked in a faint voice. "Your face is so smooth! You look like the man I married forty years ago!"

Hearing this, the old man put his hands to his face. It was just as his wife had said.

He was no longer an old man—he became young again!

He sat down to think. "How can this be?" he wondered.

After a while he slapped his knee. "It must be the spring water I drank."

The old woman was very puzzled and demanded that her husband tell about what had happened.

When he had finished, she began to cry. "It's a wonderful thing, what has happened to you. But everyone will think it strange that you have such an old wife."

The man just laughed at her. "Not to worry. Come back to the fountain with me. You can become young again, too. Then we'll both be young together! Nobody will say that you are married to a man too young."

As soon as it became bright enough the next day, the man led his old wife to the spring.

She drank a few sips of the spring water and fell into a deep sleep. When she woke, her young husband was sitting by her side. She was a pretty young woman again.

Once young again, the couple lived together even more happily than they had before.

But their mean neighbor became unbearably jealous. "I want to loose wrinkles and white hair, too! I want to be young again and live a long life!" he fumed.

He could not stand it any longer. He hurried over to the young couple's house.

"You must tell me," he shouted, "how did you become so young again?"

The couple had no reason to keep the spring a secret, so they told him about what had happened.

The selfish neighbor hurried to the mountain forest alone, mumbling to himself as he went. He didn't come back for two days, so the young couple were worried and went to look for him.

When they reached the place where the spring had been, all they found was a little puddle of water. Then they heard a very loud, high-pitched cry coming from a nearby rock. When they looked, they saw a naked baby lying on top of their neighbor's clothes.

The young man and woman laughed. "He drank so much of the spring water he became too young for his clothes!" They took the baby home with them and raised him as though he were their very own.

With their kind, loving care, the baby grew into a nice, helpful young boy.

The Dog and the Cat

In a small riverside village, there lived an old tavern keeper. He lived all alone with a dog and a cat that never left his side. The dog guarded the door to the house, and the cat kept the storeroom free of rats. People would come from beyond the other side of the village to drink his wine, and travelers often asked for a jug to bring with them on their journey.

There was something strange about his wine, though. No matter how much he sold, he never seemed to run out. His neighbors were quite curious about this, for they never saw any wine delivered to the tavern and they knew that he didn't make any himself. It was a secret that he shared only with his dog and cat.

He had not always been a tavern keeper. Many years ago he had worked as a ferryman, ferrying people back and forth across a river that flowed alongside what later became his tavern.

Just as he arrived at the door of his house one cold rainy night, he heard an old man speaking to him. "Please, sir, could you spare a bowl of wine? It would help take the chill out of these old bones of mine," he said.

"Come in," said he. "My wine jug is almost empty, but you're welcome to what's left." He emptied his jug into a bowl. But the stranger poured some of what was in the bowl back into the jug and then drank all that he could.

"You have been most kind," said the stranger, then he got to his feet. "Please take this as a token of my appreciation," he said, handing him a piece of amber. "Keep it in your wine jug and it will never get dry."

He turned the amber over and over in his hands for a while and then, with a laugh, dropped it into his wine jug. He thought he would have to pick it out when he filled the jug the next day. Not much later he got thirsty, "There must be at least a drop," he told himself, picking up the jug. What a surprise he got when he found the jug was full!

He poured a small bowl and drank sip. It was the sweetest, richest wine he had ever tasted. He drank the whole bowl and promptly poured another, but the jug stayed full no matter how often he checked.

He was overjoyed. "How wonderful! Now I can open a tavern! No more ferrying back and forth across that river for this old man!" He did open his tavern, and that is how it all came about. People came from all over to taste his wine.

One day he picked up his jug to serve a traveler, he discovered that it was completely empty. He shook it furiously, but it didn't make any sound. He was dumbfounded. "It must have come out while I was pouring someone wine! My goodness! What shall I do?"

The dog and the cat noticed his sadness and desperately sniffed around the shop to find the amber.

"I'm sure I could find it if I could only pick up the scent," the cat talked to the dog.

The dog was thinking hard too. "Let's go through every house in the neighborhood. We have to find it," he said.

So they began their search, determined to find the lost amber for their master. It wasn't easy, and at times their search was even quite dangerous. When the water froze, they crossed the river to sniff through the houses on the other side. All winter long they crossed back and forth across the river to find the amber. Together they searched and sniffed every corner of every house and shop for miles around.

One day, when the river was beginning to thaw, the cat caught the scent of the amber in a box atop a large chest. But the cat and the dog didn't know what to do. If the cat pushed it off the chest, someone would hear them. And the box was too big for the dog to carry in his mouth.

"Let's ask the rats to help us," suggested the dog. "They could gnaw a hole in the box and get the amber out for us." "But do you really expect them to help us?" the cat asked.

"It sounds like a far-fetched idea, but we could promise not to bother them for ten years," said the dog.

Surprisingly, the rats consented. They welcomed the chance to live free of the fear of dogs and cats. It took several days for them to gnaw a hole large enough for a small rat to get inside the box and carry out the amber.

The dog and the cat thanked the rats and headed for the river, taking turns carrying the amber in their mouths.

"Oh no!" cried the cat when they got to the river's edge. "The ice has melted, but I can't swim." The cat was desperately scared of the water. "Yes, I know. That's a problem," said the dog. "I have an idea," he said after a while. "I'll carry you on my back and you'll carry the amber in your mouth." The cat was scared, but there didn't seem to be much choice. He took the amber in his mouth, then climbed onto the dog's back.

The dog walked into the water and began swimming. Once floating in the water he asked, "Are you holding on to that amber tightly?" The cat heard the dog's question, but couldn't answer with the amber in his mouth.

A little bit later, the dog asked again. “Do you still have the amber?” The cat wanted to tell the dog not to worry, but didn’t want to loose the amber, either.

“Are you holding on tightly?” “Have you dropped it?” “Is it still in your mouth?” The dog asked over and over, but of course the cat could not respond.

As they came near the other side of the river, the dog shouted, “Why don’t you answer me? Don’t you still have the amber?” The cat was so frustrated, it accidentally answered the dog. “Of course I still have it!” he said, and the amber fell into the water.

The dog was so angry he shook the cat off his back. Somehow the cat made it to shore, at which point the dog chased him until he finally ran up a tree.

The dog returned to the river and swam to the spot where the cat dropped the amber.

At that moment he noticed the scent of the amber. The smell was coming from a fish caught by a fisherman just a little ways downstream.

The fisherman never noticed when the dog stole a fish from his catch. Carefully the dog carried the fish home to the master.

"That's a good dog," he said when the dog dropped the fish at his feet. "We needed something to eat." When he cut the fish open, he almost fainted. "I can't believe it! It's my amber! My amber!" he said jumping for joy.

He locked the amber in a chest and went out to buy a jug of wine so he could open his tavern again.

But when he returned and opened the chest he was surprised to find two money pouches instead of one, two jackets instead of one, and two combs instead of one. Everything he had in the chest had doubled. This is how he learned that the secret of the amber was that it doubled everything it touched.

After that he became richer that he had ever dreamed possible. He made sure that the dog was well fed and often wondered what had happened to his other four-footed companion.

As for the dog, he never killed a rat again. Instead he chased away every cat that crossed his path.

The Tortoise and the Hare

Long ago, the Dragon King of the East Sea became very ill. The court physician read the king's pulse and then, looking very grim, said to the Dragon King, "Your Majesty, you must eat the fresh raw liver of a hare. That is a land animal. Unfortunately it is the only thing that will cure Your Majesty's disease."

"Send for a hare liver at once," said the Dragon King, turning to his chief court minister.

"But Your Majesty, we sea creatures can't live on land," replied the minister. All the others present nodded in agreement.

"Nonsense, there is one among you who can," said the Dragon King.

"And that is I," said a tortoise, slowly making his way to the minister. "Being a tortoise, I can survive on land. I would be honored to be able to fetch a hare to cure Your Majesty."

The Dragon King ordered the court artists to paint a picture of a hare for the tortoise. And in no time at all he had in his hands a detailed picture of the long-legged, long-eared creature. Tucking it safely inside his shell, the tortoise departed on his quest.

Sometimes swimming, sometimes floating, he eventually came to land. He looked in all directions for a place from which to watch out for a hare, eventually settling in a small mountain overlooking some farmland.

It was a lovely spring day. Birds and butterflies filled the sky and many animals passed below, but not one looked like the animal in the drawing he had.

Exhausted, he stretched out his long neck and scanned his immediate surroundings. As he did his eyes came to rest on a patch of clovers. Much to his delight, the reason for his long journey was in the middle of the patch nibbling the tender leaves and flowers. He cleared his voice and took a deep breath.

"Excuse me," he called.

The hare quickly hopped away. But being a very curious hare, he sneaked up behind the tortoise and, thumping on its shell, said in a loud voice, “Who are you and where do you come from?” “Oh! It’s you, Mr. Hare. I’ve heard so much about you. I’m delighted to make your acquaintance. Utterly delighted, I’m Tortoise. I’m from the East Sea.” The hare was pleased to hear that the tortoise had heard of him. “Yes, right. I’m pleased to meet you, too. But may I ask what you are doing here so far from home?”

“I’m out sightseeing. You see, I had heard so many good things about the land you live on that I wanted to see it myself. It is nice indeed, but it doesn’t compare with my home, which is truly a world of beauty. Have you ever visited the kingdom at the bottom of the sea?” asked the tortoise.

“No, I haven’t,” said the hare.

“That’s too bad. I would have thought a creature that moves as fast as you would have been everywhere,” said the tortoise, trying to flatter the hare.

"Well, I have often thought that I would like to visit there sometime. "I've been to many places, and it would round out my travels," boasted the hare.

"Then come along with me. I'll show you the most fantastic sights of our fair kingdom," cajoled the tortoise.

"But I heard it was impossible to go there," said the hare with great surprise, "that's what everyone says." "Yes, it is," said the tortoise, "unless of course you travel with me. I will show you things more splendid than you could ever dream about. Just think of the

marvelous adventures you would be able to recount to your friends." "Yes, indeed. That would be something to tell my friends," mused the hare. "Just imagine how envious ..."

"Enough! Enough!! I'll go! I'll go!!" exclaimed the hare.

"Just hop on my back," said the tortoise, trying hard to contain his excitement.

The tortoise crawled back to the seashore with the hare boasting about his travels and exploits all the way. "Now hold on tight to my shell," said the tortoise and dove into the sea. He swam straight down.

Finally, with the hare holding his breath all the way, they arrived at the kingdom at the very bottom of the sea. The tortoise led the hare to a room beautifully decorated with coral and shells and left him there, saying that he would be back soon.

The hare waited there in his guest room until a school of swordfish and a cuttlefish came and told him to come with them.

"His Majesty has been expecting you," said the cuttlefish.

"He's been expecting me?" asked the hare.

"Of course. He's been anxiously awaiting your arrival," said the cuttlefish to the amusement of the swordfish.

"Why?" asked the hare in astonishment.

"Because of your great liver," said the cuttlefish, wrapping a long tentacle around the hare.

"Your great liver," he chuckled.

"But I don't understand," said the hare, beginning to feel uncomfortable.

"In time, in time," said the cuttlefish.

Presently they came to a large door covered with pearls.

"Now be quite," said the cuttlefish, just as the door swung open. "Your Majesty, King of the Sea and all that reside therein," his voice boomed out, "here is the hare." The hare looked up and almost fell over in shock at finding himself there before the Dragon King. He was so scared that his long pink ears shook in fear.

"Welcome to my kingdom," said the Dragon King in a hoarse voice. "I'm very sick and the tortoise brought you here so that I can eat your liver. It is the only known cure for my illness. But please do not feel sad. Your death will not be in vain. It is for a good cause. Consider yourself fortunate to have died for a worthy cause, rather than as the prey of a hunter or some beast of the forest. Now prepare yourself to die a noble death."

The hare knew that he had to remain calm. He bowed deeply to the Dragon King and then, to have time to think of a way to save himself, he bowed to all the nobles surrounding the Dragon King and to the swordfish guards standing ready to slay him.

"Your Majesty," he finally said, bowing to the Dragon King again. "I would gladly sacrifice myself to save your life. Unfortunately, slitting open my belly now would not do either of us any good because my liver is not with me." "What?" roared the Dragon King. "Do you expect me to believe that?"

"But it's true, Your Majesty. Since my liver has special curing powers, it is always in great demand. Therefore I use it mostly at night, and then keep it hidden in the daytime. If Tortoise had only told me of Your Majesty's illness before, I would have gladly brought it."

"Do you think I am a fool?" asked the Dragon King. "It is impossible to take one's liver out at will." Then he turned to his court ministers, "Isn't that right?"

"Yes, Your Majesty, completely impossible," they chorused.

"Look, Your Majesty, look at my mouth. No other creature can take its liver out at will. That's why my upper lip is spilt," said the hare.

The Great Hall was silent. "Now, if it would please Your Majesty, I would gladly go get my liver if Tortoise will take me home."

"Tortoise," the Dragon King finally spoke, "take the hare to get his liver. And hurry."

The tortoise and the hare departed at once. The hare danced for joy when the tortoise at long last crawled out of the water. He laughed and laughed until he thought his liver really would pop right out his mouth.

"I know you must be happy to be home for one final visit," said the tortoise after catching his breath. "But please make haste and get your liver. We really must hurry back to the Dragon King."

"You stupid tortoise! Despite your years, you actually believe I can remove my liver. Ha-ha-ha! You thought you would trick me, but I have had the last laugh!" said the hare. He hopped away, laughing boisterously.

The tortoise wept as he thought about his dying King. He knew there wasn't enough time for him to capture another hare.

Suddenly a god with a long white beard appeared and said in a resonant voice, "Don't despair.

I will help you, for you are one of great faithfulness. Take these ginseng roots to your king. They will cure his illness and restore his health."

The tortoise thanked him and hurried back to the Dragon King's palace with the ginseng roots. The Dragon King ate them and became well immediately.

Now better, he gave the tortoise the position of Special Attendant and made him the highest-ranking minister in his court.

The Vanity of the Rat

Once there was a rat couple who had only one daughter. As they had no other children, they doted on her.

When it came time for their daughter to get married, they wanted only the best husband for her. They thought about all the rats they knew, but none of them was quite good enough for their daughter.

One day Mr. Rat said to his wife, "I know who will make a perfect husband for our little darling, the sun." "The sun?" asked Mrs. Rat. "Why do you think the sun will be a good husband for her?" "Because there is none more powerful in the world than the sun." "Yes, yes. The sun is the most powerful. He's bright as well. Let's ask him at once," said Mrs. Rat happily.

The two went out into their garden where the sun was beaming down. "Oh, Mr. Sun!" they called, trying to keep their eyes open as they looked up into the sky.

"Yes, what can I do for you?" replied the sun.

"Should you accept, my wife and I would like to offer you our daughter's hand in marriage," said Mr. Rat proudly.

"I'm honored," said the sun, "but why do you want me to marry her?" "Because you are so powerful and magnificent," said Mr. Rat while Mrs. Rat nodded in agreement.

"Well, I'm pleased that you think so highly of me," said the sun. "But I must confess that there is one that is more powerful than me." "Who might that be?" asked Mr. Rat with surprise.

"Why Mr. Cloud, of course! I am powerless when he covers me." "Yes, so true," said Mr. Rat, nodding over and over.

"Come, my dear," he said, taking his wife by the hand. "Let's go see Mr. Cloud."

They climbed up a nearby mountain over which a big, billowy cloud hung in the sky. They called to Mr. Cloud and, telling him what they had heard from the sun, offered him their daughter's hand in marriage.

Again the couple got an answer much different from what they had expected. Mr. Cloud said, "What the sun told you is correct. But I am powerless when I meet Mr. Wind. Wherever he blows, I must go."

"Yes, yes. Of course. Of course," said Mr. and Mrs. Rat, and they set out to find Mr. Wind.

Coming down the mountain, they found Mr. Wind in a grove of pines.

"I am strong," he told them on hearing their story. "I can make a big tree topple over or blow down a house. I can even shake up the ocean. But try as I may, I cannot budge a stone Buddha. I am powerless before a stone Buddha."

"Then we'll just have to ask a stone Buddha," said Mr. Rat. So Mr. and Mrs. Rat hurried on down the trail to talk to a stone Buddha standing near their village.

"Well, I'm flattered that you want me to marry your daughter," said Mr. Stone Buddha, "but I don't think I'm right for her either. I am indeed strong and Mr. Wind can't move me, but I am by no means the strongest of them all. There is one that can make me fall over quite easily. The very thought is just making me shake already." "Please, Mr. Stone Buddha, please tell us who," said Mr. Rat.

"None other than you and your cousins, the moles," said Mr. Stone Buddha. "You and your cousins are really strong. Why, if one of you burrows under my feet, I'll topple right over and smash my face. I'm no match for you." "Thank you. You've been very helpful," said Mr. Rat, trying to hide his embarrassment.

After the long search for a suitable suitor, the rat's daughter finally married a rat.

The Firedogs

Once upon a time there was a land known as the Kingdom of Darkness. It was pitch black and completely without any light at all. In the dark its people raised large, fierce dogs called "firedogs."

The king of the Kingdom of Darkness was genuinely concerned about the sad and depressing state in his kingdom. He wanted it to be bright, just like other kingdoms.

One day as he sat on his throne thinking about what he could do to fix the situation, he suddenly slapped his knee and smiled. He had an idea.

"Here boy! Come here!" he called to his fiercest fire dog. "This land is too dark, and life here is too hard. So steal the sun and bring it here so that we can have some light shine on us."

"As you wish, Your Highness," said the dog. "I will go at once and fetch the sun."

Then the dog flew off into the sky.

The fire dog traveled for several days without stopping to rest.

Only when he was far enough from the kingdom that was his home did he see the sun.

Just as he had heard from dogs that had seen the sun, the closer he got, the brighter and hotter it was. His hair got burnt a little on the ends, but he moved on anyway.

Just when it was almost too hot to endure any longer, he decided that he was close enough to bite the sun.

Firedogs are usually very brave. But this fire dog was more than a little frightened at this point. He had never seen anything so bright and he had never been so hot. He closed his eyes, opened his mouth wide and bit down on the sun.

"Yaaaouch! That's HOT!" yelped the fire dog, jumping back away from the hot mass.

Hot as it was though, he didn't want to disappoint the king. "I'll try again. I'll get it this time," he told himself. He closed his eyes very tight and bit down hard on the sun again. "Oh! It's too hot! It's too hot!" he cried, spitting it out again.

Sweating heavily all the while, the fire dog tried over and over to sink his teeth into the burning sun, but every single time he had to spit it out. After numerous unsuccessful tries, the dog finally gave up and returned home.

"You should be ashamed, coming home empty-handed like this," said the king to the exhausted fire dog, who was barely able to stand up straight. "If you couldn't get the sun, at least you could have brought the moon."

"So true, Your Highness. I will bring you the moon without fail," said the dog, and with those words he flew off to steal the moon.

Finally, after several days, the fire dog saw the moon. The closer he got to it, the colder it became. But he flew on for he was determined to take the moon to the king.

As soon as he was close enough, the fire dog closed his eyes and bit down hard on the moon.

“Yikes! How cold!” he cried, and let go of the moon. He bit down even harder the next time, but he still could not hold on because his teeth were hurting from the cold. He tried repeatedly until his jaw was almost frozen stiff and was forced to go home again, this time without the moon.

The king was furious. “You there!” He called to his second fiercest fire dog. “You go steal the sun. And if you can’t get the sun, get the moon.”

But the second fiercest fire dog of the kingdom also retuned with his mouth empty. The king was determined that he would find some light for his dark kingdom.

He sent a third fire dog and a fourth and a fifth. All failed, but he never gave up hope, and neither did the many kings that came after him.

It is said that eclipses are caused when firedogs from the Kingdom of Darkness try to bite the sun and the moon.

The Two Brothers

In times gone by there lived two brothers. Their loving, kind ways to treat each other were the talk of everyone in the valley where they lived. They took care of their widowed mother until her death. Later they divided everything evenly among the two of them without argument.

Together they worked very hard all through the day to produce as much as they could from their fields. Every autumn they would have the largest harvest in the village.

One late autumn evening, after they had spent the whole afternoon dividing up the last of the rice harvest, the older brother thought to himself, "My younger brother got married just a few months ago and has many expenses these days. I think I will put a sack of my portion of the rice in his storehouse and not tell him. He would never accept it knowingly."

So late that night, he put a sack of rice on his back and carried it to his brother's storeroom.

The next day, while tidying up the storeroom in his own house, the older brother was surprised to find he still had the same number of sacks of rice as he had before.

"That's strange," he thought. "I'll just take another one to him tonight when it gets dark."

Late that night, he carried another sack of rice to his brother's house.

The next morning he was again surprised to find he had same number of sacks as before. He stood there confused until evening. In the end, he decided to try and take yet another sack to the house of his younger brother.

After a late dinner he loaded the rice on his back and set out for his brother's house. It was a full moon and he could see the path quite clearly. He could also see a man carrying something bulky while hurrying down the path in his direction.

"Why brother!" they both called out at the same time.

The two brothers put down their sacks and laughed long and hard, for now they knew that it was nothing other than brotherly love that had caused all the confusion.

The younger brother thought his older brother could use the rice because he had a larger family. And these two brothers lived happily ever after working hard and doing many good things together.

The Tiger and the Dried Persimmon

Once upon a time in a valley deep in the mountains, there lived a huge tiger. He always walked around boasting about his strength.

"I dare anyone to try and match my strength," he would say. When the other animals of

the mountain heard him, they all ran away.

One winter, the snow piled up so high that it took the tiger two days to dig his way out of his cave. He was near starving when he crawled out of his cave to look for food, but the snow covered everything in sight.

"Oh, no!" the tiger mumbled. "How can I find something to eat?" He kept getting stuck in the snow as he wandered around the mountain in search of food.

Somehow, by the time darkness fell, he had reached the village which lay at the foot of the mountain. He poked around until he found a quiet little barn by a farmhouse. A fat cow was sleeping inside, snoring loudly.

"I think I'll have that cow!" exclaimed the tiger. "I have always liked beef!" he said, licking his chops.

Just at that moment, the tiger heard a small child crying inside the house.

"Eh! What's that noise?" thought the tiger. He sneaked up to the room where the child was crying. Inside the room, the child's mother was trying to make him stop crying. "Oh, look! There's a monster!" she said, "You had better stop crying, or he'll come here and get you!"

But the child kept on crying. So this time the mother said, "There's a tiger outside! If you don't stop crying, he'll come and eat you up!" She had not really seen the tiger. She was only trying to make the child stop crying.

When the tiger heard this, he naturally thought that the mother had seen him looking at them. "How can she know I am here?" he wondered. I should be more careful.

Now the child was crying even louder, and this made the tiger angry. He didn't like the idea of a little child not being afraid of a tiger. The child cried and cried. Nothing could scare the child into silence.

Finally the mother tried something different. She reached into a cabinet and pulled out something for him. "Look! A dried persimmon!" she said.

The child immediately stopped crying and started eating the persimmon.

The tiger had heard all of this from outside the room and was very surprised. But he had not actually seen what the mother had given to the child.

"A persimmon?" he thought. "A persimmon must be a very scary beast indeed and it must be more powerful and frightening than I am, since I didn't scare the child at all. I'd better leave here before the persimmon tries to eat me!"

The tiger walked very quietly back to the barn. He was only worried about being heard, as it was now completely dark and quiet outside.

As he arrived at the barn, something big and black crept through the door. The black shape walked right up to where the tiger was trying to hide and not be seen. It reached down and stroked the tiger's back.

Then it said, "This one's really healthy and fat!"

The tiger was so scared that it couldn't move.

The big black thing that the tiger thought was a persimmon was actually a cow thief. But it was so dark inside the barn that the thief couldn't see very well. He thought the furry tiger was the cow. The tiger didn't resist when the thief gently led him outside.

Once outside the barn, the thief reached down and patted the tiger again, but this time he noticed that what he felt was not cow fur. When he looked closely and saw the tiger, he was so scared that he froze where he stood.

The tiger, on the other hand, thought that the persimmon had gotten him for sure. He closed his eyes and believed he was on his last breath.

The thief was too afraid to move, so he just stood still next to the tiger, hoping it wouldn't notice him. The tiger thought that the persimmon must have been distracted by something. He tried to jump free and run away. But when the thief felt the tiger start to move, he thought that the tiger was going to eat him alive. To save himself he jumped onto the tiger's back and held on for dear life.

The frightened tiger jumped up and down and ran around in circles, trying to throw the thief from his back. But this made the thief hold on all that much tighter.

Next, the tiger took off, running wildly. Strong as a persimmon may be, it will surely fall if I run as fast as I can. The tiger ran with all of his strength. Even with the thief on his back, he was soon out of the village and near the base of his mountain.

Up near the ridge of the mountain, it was just light enough for the thief to see a branch hanging over the path. He reached up and grabbed the branch. Lucky for him, the tiger ran out from beneath him.

The tiger was so scared of the "persimmon" that he kept running and didn't look back. At first, he didn't even know that the thief was gone. He was too tired and frightened to notice. Eventually he noticed that his back felt lighter, so he stopped running and heaved a great sigh of relief.

"Whew!" he sighed. "That was close! Today I was nearly eaten by a persimmon."

The Rabbit and the Tiger

A long time ago on a sunny spring day, a little rabbit was just waking up from a very pleasant, peaceful nap in the shade of a big rock. "Ummm," he said as he stretched, "what a good nap!"

Then suddenly he heard a strange noise. It was a huge tiger just a few feet away. The tiger had been watching him taking his nap.

"What a pleasure to meet you, Rabbit," said the tiger. "I'm very hungry. I think I will eat you at once." The tiger opened his mouth wide. Its shadow was bigger than the rabbit.

"The pleasure is all mine, Tiger," said the rabbit, who was very worried and trying to think of a way to get out of the situation alive. "I must ask that you don't eat me right away. Just a second."

"Why?" growled the tiger.

"Wouldn't you like some rice cakes first? I know you are very hungry and I am too small to be a full meal for a tiger as big as you," the rabbit explained.

"Is this some kind of trick?" asked the tiger.

"I'm offended that you would even think such a thing!"

"All right then," purred the tiger. "Give me some rice cakes to eat before I finish you off. And be quick about it."

"It will only take me a second to get the rice cakes. I have some on the other side of this rock." Quickly the rabbit hopped to the other side of the rock and picked up eleven smooth white stones, then hopped back to where the tiger was waiting. The tiger was very suspicious. "These look like stones," growled the tiger, showing his teeth.

"Don't be silly," said the rabbit. "Rice cakes always look like stones until you cook them. Just wait. You'll see."

Then the rabbit hopped around gathering sticks for a fire, never leaving sight of the tiger that was lazily waiting for his meal.

When there was a nice blaze going (and this was a long time since the rabbit was trying to move as slow as he could), he put the rocks in it.

As the stones sat warming in the fire, the rabbit chatted with the tiger about things like the weather as if they were close friends. Soon the tiger no longer doubted him.

"Oh, oh," said the rabbit, "I forgot to get some soy sauce."

"Soy sauce? What's that?" asked the tiger.

"You've never heard of soy sauce?" The rabbit was now teasing the tiger. "It makes cooked rice cakes taste much better. I will get some and be right back. You watch the rice cakes so they don't burn."

"All right. Don't take all day," growled the tiger.

The rabbit hopped away as quickly as he could. As he made his escape, he looked back over his shoulder. "I'll be right back, Tiger," he called. "But promise me you won't eat any of those ten rice cakes until I come back, okay? I know there are ten in all!" Then he hopped along, laughing all the way.

The tiger sat in front of the fire getting hungrier and hungrier. The stones were getting red with heat.

As the tiger waited, he counted the "rice cakes" in the fire.

"One, two, three, four, five, six, seven, eight, nine, ten, eleven."

"Eleven?" The tiger counted again. "Eleven! That silly rabbit. Well, I'll eat just one rice cake while I wait for him to come back. He'll never know the difference."

The tiger swallowed one of the red-hot stones. He had never felt anything like the pain he would now experience. The tiger screamed and jumped and ran as the stone burned his mouth, his throat, and then his stomach. He could be heard screaming for miles.

Because of his burns, the tiger could not eat anything for many days. He just lay in bed and thought about what the rabbit had done to him.

When he was well enough to leave his cave, he was terribly hungry and terribly angry.

While he was out looking for something to eat, he ran into the rabbit again.

"How nice to see you again," the tiger growled. "Did you actually think you could get away with the cruel trick you played on me?" he said.

Then he opened his mouth wide like the last time to eat the rabbit all in one gulp.

The rabbit was confident of himself this time, so he smiled as he thought quickly. "Why are you so mad at me? There must have been some sort of misunderstanding."

The tiger did not know what to say.

"I have an idea!" said the rabbit.

"Oh, no. Not again," growled the tiger. "I won't let you trick me again!"

"Trick you? Me ... trick you? Never! In fact I was just on my way to your cave. I wanted to tell you how to catch birds just by opening your mouth."

The tiger was very hungry at this point. Just thinking about eating birds made his mouth water.

"Are you sure this isn't a trick?" he asked.

"Of course not," the rabbit reassured him. "Just trust me."

The rabbit led the tiger into the middle of a field of weeds. He looked at the tiger and told him, "Open your mouth and close your eyes for a big surprise while I chase birds in your direction." Then the rabbit hopped away.

The tiger waited as patiently as he could, with his head held high and his mouth opened wide. To pass the time he closed his eyes and thought about how good the birds would taste.

In the distance he could hear the rabbit making noises to scare the birds into his mouth. "Shoo, shoo," he heard him say. He also heard a sound that crackled and sizzled, but he did not pay much attention to it at first. Gradually the crackling sound became louder and louder. He thought the crackling was the movement of the birds he was going to lunch on.

In anticipation he opened his mouth even wider. When he didn't taste any bird meat, the tiger finally opened his eyes. That's when he saw the field full of weeds burning all around him. The clever rabbit had set it afire.

The tiger ran from the field. But to get out of the field he had to run through the fire. "Oh, no! Rabbit tricked me again," he shouted. "This time I'm lucky to be alive." The hungry tiger was so badly burned that he had to spend many very painful weeks lying in his cave.

Green Onions

The dawn of human history, people used to eat one another. This was because in those days human beings sometimes appeared in the form of cattle, and so were used for food.

This strange situation continued until one man set out in search of a better world. In his wandering he met a monk. The monk asked him the reason for his long journey.

"This world is horrible," he said. "I hate it, for men eat one another. I am on my way to seek a better world, where men may not do such evil things."

The monk knew the hearts of men so he gave the man some advice, "Your quest will be in vain, for wherever you may go, you will find that men are the same. You should go back to where you came from."

The traveler replied, "I cannot go back now, for if I do they will surely eat me. Isn't there anything I can do?"

"Try eating green onions. When you eat green onions, you change to human form, even if you start out in the form of an ox," said the monk.

The traveler hurried home. As he came close to his house, he met some of his fellow villagers. He greeted them cheerfully, "Hello there! How have you been? I haven't seen you for a while."

The villagers didn't answer him. Instead they surrounded him in the road.

"A most healthy looking ox!" said one of them, and they tied him to a post. "Let's eat him together."

Just then it happened that a young girl passed by, carrying a basket full of green onions on her head.

Somehow, while still tied to the post, he managed to snatch one. He swallowed it whole, and immediately changed into normal human form. The villagers were very sorry and surprised.

"Our dear friend. We are very sorry indeed. We didn't realize it was you."

Thank goodness he had lived to tell them all about the miraculous powers of green onions. Since then, people of all shapes and forms ate green onions, and now everyone looks like they should.

To this day it is said that the cultivation of green onions was encouraged by good people in the hope that villagers wouldn't eat each other any more.

The Green Frog

Once upon a time, there lived a green frog who would never do what his mother told him. If she told him to go to the east, he would go to the west. If she asked him to go up the mountain, he would run down to the river. He didn't obey his mother in anything.

Even when his mother had grown very old, she was still forced to worry about her son's future.

Already very old, one day she became very ill as well, and thought that she was near death. So she called her son to her bedside and said to him, "My dear son, I shall not live much longer. When I die, do not bury me on the mountain. I want to be buried by the river. Do you understand me?"

Saying this was the only way she could be sure that she would be buried on the mountain.

Soon afterwards she died. The young frog was very sad and wept bitterly. Only then did he feel remorse for the way he had treated his mother while she was still alive. He decided that from that point on he would do as his mother would have wanted and so buried her by the riverside.

Whenever it rained he worried that her grave would be washed away. Until the day he joined her in Heaven, the son sat by the river and cried whenever it rained.

To this day the green frog croaks whenever the weather is wet.

The Heavenly Maiden and the Woodcutter

Once upon a time there was a young man who lived in a village with his old mother near the foot of the Diamond Mountains. He was very poor, so in order to live, he would go up into the mountains everyday to cut firewood and sell it to his neighbors.

One day when he was cutting fire wood deep in the mountain, he heard something running in his direction over the fallen leaves. It was a terrified young deer running toward him.

When it saw him, the deer stopped and began to beg him for help. The deer said that it was in great danger, so the young bachelor helped him hide behind a tree. Then he went back to work as if nothing had happened.

Almost at once a hunter came running towards him. It took a while for the hunter to catch his breath.

"I have been chasing a deer. It ran up this way. Have you seen it?"

He stood in front of the woodcutter with his bow and arrows.

Pointing at the opposite directions from where the deer was hiding, the woodcutter smiled at him and said, “Yes, I did see a deer run through here. It came running by and went off down into the valley over there. I couldn’t say where it headed after that.”

The hunter rushed back down the mountain without even saying thank you.

Then the young deer came out from behind the tree. It also had to catch its breath because it had been forced to keep from breathing while the hunter stood there. It thanked the woodcutter for his kindness.

“You saved my life, and I am most deeply grateful to you. To repay your kindness, I will tell you something that will bring you great happiness.” Then it continued, “Go up to one of the lakes in the Diamond Mountains tomorrow afternoon before two o’clock. When you get there, hide yourself among the bushes by the water’s edge. After a while you will see eight

Heavenly Maidens come down from the corner of Heaven to bathe in the lakes. Before they go into the lake they will hang their silken clothes on tree branches. Without letting them see you, hide some of the clothes. Then when it comes time for them to return to Heaven, one of them will be forced to stay here on earth. You will live a happy life together and have many children. But whatever you do, don't give her back her silk garments until you have had four children."

The young man was so happy at hearing this that he never noticed that the deer had left.

The next morning the young man got up very early and climbed to one of the peaks of the Diamond Mountains, where there are eight beautiful lakes.

The young man concealed himself among the bushes and waited.

Suddenly the clouds opened and eight Heavenly Maidens came floating down to the lakes at the end of a rainbow. They talked merrily one another as they took off their clothes and hung them on the branches of pine trees. Then each jumped into the clear water of one of the eight lakes.

As they enjoyed themselves in the water, the woodcutter watched them for a while, for he was struck at their beauty. But he soon came to his senses and remembered what the deer had told him. He quietly crept into the pine trees and took the clothes of the youngest maiden.

As it got close to sunset, the Heavenly Maidens prepared to return to Heaven. They began to put on their clothes again, but the youngest maiden could not find her clothes. She would have to stay behind, for there was no other way for her to return to Heaven. The others could not wait, so they climbed up the rainbow into Heaven. The young maiden that was left behind set about searching for her clothes and soon found the young man watching her.

He begged her to forgive him. He was very kind and attentive to her, so she followed him home.

At first the Heavenly Maiden found the customs of life on earth most confusing, but she soon settled into a routine of normal human life.

Months passed, and she gave birth to a son. They were very happy, and when their second child was born they were happier than ever.

Then one day the wife asked the husband to return her Heavenly clothing. "I have born you two children. Can't you trust me now?" The man refused, for he was afraid that she might carry his children off with her, one in each arm.

When their third child was born she again asked for the clothes. She served him delicious food and wine, trying to get him in a good mood. "My dearest husband! Please just let me see my clothes. I can hardly betray you now, can I? We have three children now!"

The young man was sympathetic to his wife's feelings, and now showed her the clothes that he had kept hidden so long. But just as the deer had warned, when she put them on again she regained her magic power, and at once went up to the sky, holding one child between her legs and one in each arm.

The young man was very angry at himself for not listening to what the deer had told him. He was very sad and lonely, but there didn't seem to be anything he could do. He went out to the mountain and sat at the same place where he had seen the deer, hoping that it might reappear.

The deer did come, and it listened to the young man's sad story. Then the deer spoke, "Since the day you hid the Heavenly Maiden's clothes, none of them have bathed there anymore. If you want to see your wife and children again, then you will have to go where they are. Tomorrow morning go to the same lake and wait until you see a gourd come down from Heaven on a rope. They drop it to fetch water from the lake so that they can bathe up in Heaven. Get in before it gets filled with water. That is the only way you will be able to see your family again."

The woodcutter took the deer's advice and was able to go up to Heaven. When he arrived, the Heavenly Maidens took him before the Heavenly King. It was there before the king that he met his family, for his wife was a princess of the Heavenly King.

The king permitted him to stay, and so he stayed to live in the Heavenly Kingdom. He ate the most delicious food, wore the most beautiful clothes, and didn't have a single worry.

After a while though, he began to think of his mother. He had left her all alone on the earth below, so he told his wife that he would like to go and visit her once.

She begged him not to go, for she knew that he would not be able to return to Heaven again. But he persisted in his request and promised that he would find a way to return. The princess saw that there was nothing she could do to keep him from going.

"I will get a dragon-horse. It will take you down to earth in the blink of an eye. But whatever you do, do not dismount from it. If your feet touch the ground, you will never be able to come back to me."

The woodcutter mounted the dragon-horse and went down to see his mother.

His mother was very happy to see her son after such a long time. They talked all day, but when he said goodbye, still mounted on the dragon-horse, his mother said, "I have cooked some pumpkin porridge for you. Have some before you leave."

He didn't want to disappoint his mother, so took the bowl she offered him. But the bowl was so hot that he dropped it on the horse's back. The horse jumped violently, throwing him to the ground. Then it flew up into the sky and disappeared.

The woodcutter never went back to Heaven and spent the rest of his days looking up at the sky and missing his wife and children.

A Grain of Millet

One day, a young man was on his way to Seoul to compete for a position in the king's government. He went to an innkeeper and gave him a grain of millet. "This is very valuable," he said, "so guard it carefully till I ask for it back."

In the morning he asked the innkeeper to give him his grain of millet back. "I can't," replied the innkeeper, "A rat ate it up last night." "Then bring me the rat!" said the young man.

The innkeeper was not lying, and somehow managed to find the rat and gave it to the young man, who then departed on his way with the rat in hand.

The next evening he stayed at another inn and handed the rat to the innkeeper. "This rat is most important," he said. "Please look after it for me till I need it again."

In the morning the young man asked the innkeeper to give him his rat. "A cat ate it in the night," replied the innkeeper, so this time the young man set out carrying the cat.

Again he entrusted the owner of the inn he slept in with his precious cargo. In the morning the innkeeper told him that it had been kicked to death by a horse. So the young man demanded the horse, and amazingly the innkeeper gave it to him because he couldn't help but doing as he demanded.

Then he set out again with the horse tightly in his grip. But the next morning he was told that an ox had gored it to death. So he took the ox instead and drove it all the way to Seoul.

Again he stayed at an inn, and left the ox in the care of the innkeeper. But the son of the innkeeper sold the ox to a government minister by mistake. This time the young man demanded that the innkeeper bring him the minister.

So the innkeeper was obliged to go to the minister and humbly explain what had happened. "If he has the nerve to think he can summon me, he must be an interesting fellow," said the minister. "Bring him to me at once."

The young man was led to the house of the minister. "Give me my ox back," he demanded at once.

"I'm afraid it's already been eaten," replied the minister.

"Then bring me whoever ate it," the young man persisted stubbornly.

The minister was most impressed by the young man's fearless and persistent character, so he offered his daughter in marriage.

General Pumpkin

Long ago, there lived a rich couple who had only one son. Their son had an enormous appetite and was particularly fond of pumpkins. Since they were rich and he was their only child, his parents got all the pumpkins they could for him to eat.

They planted pumpkins in all their fields and bought more from the neighbors and even more at the market. His mother made pumpkin cake, pumpkin pudding, pumpkin soup, and pumpkin porridge. He ate nothing but pumpkins. He would eat a bagful of pumpkins at every meal, and yet he always complained that he was hungry for more pumpkins.

His parents spent so much money to feed him that in the end they had no more money.

To make matters worse, their son, the pumpkin eater, used to break wind so often and so violently that in the end the villagers refused to put up with him any longer. They had become fed up with the smell and thunderous rumblings. One day they drove him away from the village.

So the pumpkin eater wandered from village to village begging for pumpkins. People

who had not heard of him often gave him work, for he looked very big and strong. They especially liked him because he did not ask for money, but only for pumpkins. After a few days, though, he would be sent away when people saw how filthy he was.

One day he came to a big Buddhist temple in the mountains. It was a very rich and famous temple with many priests, but it was also so famous that it often fell victim to a band of robbers led by Hairy Jang. Jang used to disguise himself as a local temple visitor and go to the temple to spy and formulate a plan. Then at night he would lead his band into the temple, raid it, and carry off all the valuables they could lay their hands on.

When the Abbot saw the pumpkin eater standing before the gate of the temple, he went and welcomed him warmly, for he thought that the gigantic stranger could help keep away the robbers. He led him into the temple and, bowing humbly before him, asked him what his favorite food was.

"You do look a strong man indeed, young friend," he said. "What is your favorite food?"

"I eat nothing but pumpkins," he answered. "You had better cook as many as you can for me, say ... a whole kettleful."

So the monks of the temple entertained him with a whole kettle of pumpkin porridge, and then brought him another whole meal of pumpkin cakes. Having fed him, they asked him to help should the robbers attack the temple again.

That evening Jang came to the temple. When he saw the pumpkin eater's meal of pumpkins being prepared, he asked a monk, "Are you having a party tonight?"

"Yes. We're having General Pumpkin as our special guest."

"How many soldiers has he?" asked Jang.

The Abbot smiled. "He has come alone, and will eat them all himself." The robber chief was astounded to hear this, and decided to stay the night in the temple so that he might take a closer look at the general. Some of the monks recognized Jang and went to tell the Abbot, who told the pumpkin eater that the man who had been looting the temple was staying in the next room. The young man told the priests to wait until midnight, then to take their drums and hide in every corner of the temple, and also to make sure no candles remained lit in the temple. Meanwhile all Jang's men had gathered outside the temple and were now trying to break in.

Suddenly, out of the stillness of the night, there came a deep rumble. The air was filled with an unbearable stench. General Pumpkin had broken wind. A violent wind blew down the brick wall surrounding the temple. Jang and his men tried to run away, but whichever way they turned they were met with the sound of drums. In the end, Jang died in this strange warfare, and his band was crushed under the falling bricks of the wall.

The Abbot thanked the pumpkin eater for his assistance and invited him to stay in the temple as long as he desired. He lived there for many years and was given all the pumpkins he could eat.

Each year the monks planted a large area of the temple fields with pumpkins just for their special guest.